The Magic Key

Lost in the Jungle

Story by Roderick Hunt

Illustrations by Alex Brychta

OXFORD

UNIVERSITY PRESS

Titles in the series

Tomorrow was Mum's birthday.

Chip had a box of chocolates for her.

Kipper had made her a monkey at school.

Biff didn't know what to get.

Biff asked Anneena's mum to help her buy
a plant.
They went into a big greenhouse.
The greenhouse was hot, and it was
full of plants.

'What a lot of plants!' said Biff. 'It's like a
jungle in here.
I don't know which one to buy.'
In the end she found one that she liked.
'I'll get this one for Mum,' she said.

The next day was Mum's birthday and the
children gave her their presents.
Mum liked them all.
'Thank you,' she said. 'What a lovely plant, Biff!'

Dad had a present for Mum.

It was a plant.

'I didn't know Biff had a plant as well,'
said Dad.

'I don't mind a bit,' said Mum.

Anneena came to play with Biff and Chip.

'This is from my mum,' she said.

Wilma's mum came round with a plant too.

'Thank you,' said Mum. 'I love plants.

It's quite like a jungle in here.'

The children went to play in Biff's room.

Anneena looked at the little house.

'Can we have a magic adventure?' she asked.

'We can if the key glows,' said Kipper.

Just then the key did begin to glow.

The magic took them into a jungle.

The jungle was full of plants.

'It's wonderful,' said Biff. 'Look at that one; it's ten times bigger than the one I gave Mum.'

They saw a monkey up a tree.

It jumped up and down on the branch.

'That monkey looks cross,' said Kipper. 'I don't
think it likes us.'

'It looks like you,' said Chip.

The monkey was angry with the children.

It shook the branch.

Then it began to throw things at them.

'We can't stay here,' said Biff. 'Come on.'

They ran through the jungle, but suddenly
Chip stopped.
'Oh no!' he said, 'Look at this.'
There was a big snake in the way.
'We can't go this way,' said Chip. 'Come on.'

They came to a river.

There were alligators asleep on the bank.

'Don't wake them up,' said Kipper. 'They might get angry.'

'They might like you for dinner,' said Biff.

Suddenly they fell into a big net.

It pulled them up in the air.

'Oh help!' called Anneena. 'We're in a trap.'

The children were hanging in the net.

The net was a trap to catch animals.

'Help! Help!' called the children.

'Let us down!' called Kipper.

A man and a lady came out of the trees.

They were explorers.

'Don't worry,' said the lady, 'we'll soon get
you down.'

'What are you doing in the jungle?' asked the
man. 'Are you lost?'
'Yes,' said Biff. 'I think we are.'
'So are we,' said the lady, 'but then we
have been lost for years.'

She showed them a picture.

'We are looking for this place,' she said.

'It's called the Lost City.

Nobody lives there.

It's been lost for years and years.'

The children liked the explorers.

They wanted to help them find the Lost City.

'Maybe we can find it today,' said Kipper.

'I don't think so,' said the man.

'We have been looking for years.'

They came to a rope bridge.

'Maybe the Lost City is over there,' said Biff.

'Let's go and see.'

They began to cross the bridge.

'I hope it's safe,' said Kipper.

They found a boat on the bank of the river.

The boat was full of water.

'Oh good!' said the explorers. 'We lost
this boat years ago.'

They got in the boat and paddled down
the river.

'Look at all the alligators!' said Chip. 'I hope
it's not their dinner time.'

They came to a waterfall.

The explorer could not stop the boat.

The paddle had broken.

'Look out!' he called. 'We're going

to get wet.'

The boat went through the waterfall.
'Oh help,' said Anneena, 'I don't like
getting wet.'
'Think of the alligators,' said Chip. 'It's
better than getting eaten!'

Behind the waterfall there were some steps.
The steps went up and up for a long way.
Nobody could see how far they went.
'This may be the way to the Lost City,' said
the lady. 'Come on.'

As they climbed the steps, some bats flew
past them.
'If this is the way to the city, I can see how it
got lost,' said Anneena. 'It's such
a long way up.'

'It's the Lost City!' shouted the explorers.
'We have found it at last.'
The man threw his hat in the air and his wife
jumped up and down.
'I knew we'd find it today,' said Kipper.

Nobody had been in the city for years.

There were plants and trees everywhere.

Biff pulled a plant out of a wall.

'This is like the one I gave Mum,' she said.

They went to a big building and they
opened the doors.

'Oh look!' they all gasped.

Everything inside the building was made
of gold.

The floor was gold and the walls were gold.

There were some gold steps that went up to a

gold throne.

'What a wonderful place!' said Anneena.

'There's gold everywhere.'

Kipper sat on the gold throne.

A monkey jumped down behind him.

'Look at me!' he said.

'Look at the monkey behind Kipper,' said Biff.

'Which one is the monkey?' asked Chip.

Suddenly, the key began to glow.

'It's time to go home,' said Chip.

'Goodbye,' said the explorers. 'Thank you for helping us find the Lost City.'

'I wish we had a magic key,' said the man.

The magic took the children home.

Biff still had the plant she found in the lost city.

'I'll put it in Mum's jungle,' she said.

'I know where we can get a monkey too.'

Questions about the story

- What did Mum say that made the adventure start?
- Who went on this adventure?
- Where were they when they met the explorers?
- Make a list of all the animals they saw in the jungle.
- Where did they have to go before they found the Lost City?
- What do you like most about the Lost City?
- What did Chip say on page 9 and on page 30?
- Who said the same thing on page 32?
- What did they bring back from this adventure?

UNIVERSITY PRESS

Great Clarendon Street, Oxford OX2 6DP

Oxford University Press is a department of the University of Oxford.
It furthers the University's objective of excellence in research, scholarship,
and education by publishing worldwide in

Oxford New York

Athens Auckland Bangkok Bogotá Buenos Aires Calcutta Cape Town
Chennai Dar es Salaam Delhi Florence Hong Kong Istanbul Karachi
Kuala Lumpur Madrid Melbourne Mexico City Mumbai Nairobi
Paris São Paulo Shanghai Singapore Taipei Tokyo Toronto Warsaw

with associated companies in Berlin Ibadan

Oxford is a registered trade mark of Oxford University Press
in the UK and in certain other countries

British Library Cataloguing in Publication Data

Data available

ISBN 0 19 919427 0

Printed in Hong Kong